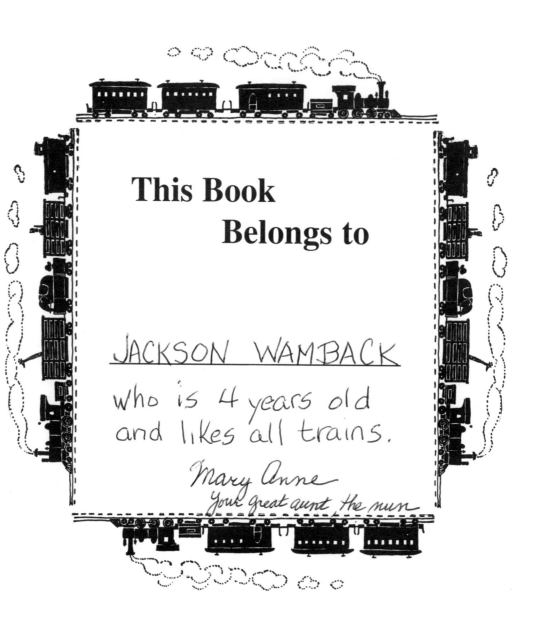

**This Book
Belongs to**

JACKSON WAMBACK

who is 4 years old
and likes all trains.

Mary Anne
Your great aunt the nun

THE LITTLE ENGINE THAT COULD

SHE WAS A HAPPY LITTLE TRAIN

THE LITTLE ENGINE THAT COULD

TRADE MARK

RETOLD BY

WATTY PIPER

PICTURES BY

LOIS L. LENSKI

•NEW·YORK•

·THE·PLATT·&·MUNK·C⍛ INC·

·PUBLISHERS·

in association with **GROSSET & DUNLAP**

THE LITTLE ENGINE THAT COULD

Chug, chug, chug. Puff, puff, puff. Ding-dong, ding-dong. The little train rumbled over the tracks. She was a happy little train for she had such a jolly load to carry. Her cars were filled full of good things for boys and girls.

There were toy animals—giraffes with long necks, Teddy bears with almost no necks at all, and even a baby elephant. Then there were dolls—dolls with blue eyes and yellow curls, dolls with brown eyes and brown bobbed heads, and the

gayest little toy clown you ever saw. And there were cars full of toy engines, aeroplanes, tops, jack-knives, picture puzzles, books, and every kind of thing boys or girls could want.

But that was not all. Some of the cars were filled with all sorts of good things for boys and girls to eat—big golden oranges, red-cheeked apples, bottles of creamy milk for their breakfasts, fresh spinach for their dinners, peppermint drops, and lollypops for after-meal treats.

The little train was carrying all these good things to the good little boys and

girls on the other side of the mountain. She puffed along happily. Then all of a sudden she stopped with a jerk. She simply

could not go another inch. She tried and she tried, but her wheels would not turn.

What were all those good little boys and girls on the other side of the mountain going to do without the jolly toys to play with and the wholesome food to eat?

"Here comes a shiny new engine," said the little clown who had jumped out of the train. "Let us ask him to help us."

So all the dolls and toys cried out together:

"Please, Shiny New Engine, do carry our train over the mountain. Our engine

has broken down, and the boys and girls on the other side will have no toys to play with and no wholesome food to eat unless you help us."

But the Shiny New Engine snorted: "I pull you? I am a Passenger Engine. I have just carried a fine big train over the mountain, with more cars than you ever dreamed of. My train had sleeping cars, with comfortable berths; a dining-car where waiters bring whatever hungry people want to eat; and parlor cars in which people sit in soft arm-chairs and look out of big plate-glass windows. I carry the likes of you? Indeed not!" And off he

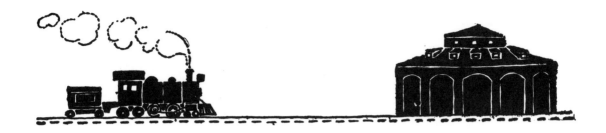

steamed to the roundhouse, where engines live when they are not busy.

How sad the little train and all the dolls and toys felt!

Then the little clown called out, "The Passenger Engine is not the only one in the world. Here is another coming, a fine big strong one. Let us ask him to help us."

The little toy clown waved his flag and the big strong engine came to a stop.

"Please, oh, please, Big Engine," cried all the dolls and toys together. "Do pull our train over the mountain. Our engine

has broken down, and the good little boys
and girls on the other side will have no
toys to play with and no wholesome food
to eat unless you help us."

But the Big Strong Engine bellowed:
"I am a Freight Engine. I have just pulled
a big train loaded with costly machines
over the mountain. These machines print

books and newspapers for grown-ups to read. I am a very important engine indeed. I won't carry the likes of you!" And

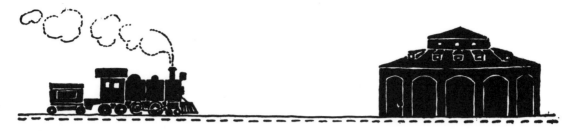

the Freight Engine puffed off indignantly to the round-house.

The little train and all the dolls and toys were very sad.

"Cheer up," cried the little toy clown. "The Freight Engine is not the only one in the world. Here comes another. He looks very old and tired, but our train is so little, perhaps he can help us."

So the little toy clown waved his flag and the dingy, rusty old engine stopped.

"Please, Kind Engine," cried all the dolls and toys together. "Do pull our train over the mountain. Our engine has broken down, and the boys and girls on the other side will have no toys to play with and no wholesome food to eat unless you help us."

But the rusty old engine sighed: "I am so tired. I must rest my weary wheels. I cannot pull even so little a train as yours over the mountain. I can not. I can not. I can not."

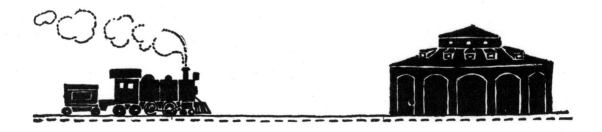

And off he rumbled to the round-house chugging, "I can not. I can not. I can not."

Then indeed the little train was very,

very sad, and the dolls and toys were ready
to cry.

But the little clown called out, "Here

is another engine coming, a little blue engine, a very little one, but perhaps she will help us."

The very little engine came chug, chugging merrily along.  When she saw the toy clown's flag, she stopped quickly.

"What is the matter, my friends?" she asked kindly.

"Oh, Little Blue Engine," cried the dolls and toys. "Will you pull us over the mountain? Our engine has broken down and the good boys and girls on the other

side will have no toys to play with and no wholesome food to eat, unless you help us. Please, please, help us, Little Blue Engine."

"I'm not very big," said the Little Blue

Engine. "They use me only for switching in the yard. I have never been over the mountain."

"But we must get over the mountain before the children awake," said all the dolls and the toys.

The very little engine looked up and saw the tears in the doll's eyes. And she thought of the good little boys and girls on the other side of the mountain who would have no toys and no wholesome food unless she helped.

Then she said, "I think I can. I think I can. I think I can." And she hitched

herself to the little train.

She tugged and pulled and pulled and tugged and slowly, slowly, slowly they started off.

The toy clown jumped aboard and all the dolls and the toy animals began to smile and cheer.

Puff, puff, chug, chug, went the little blue engine. "I think I can—I think I can

—I think I can—I think I can—I think I can—I think I can—I think I can—I think I can—I think I can."

Up, up, up. Faster and faster and faster and faster the little engine climbed until at last they reached the top of the mountain.

Down in the valley lay the city.

"Hurrah, hurrah," cried the gay little clown and all the dolls and toys. "The good little boys and girls in the city will be happy because you helped us, kind, Little Blue Engine."

And the Little Blue Engine smiled and seemed to say as she puffed steadily down the mountain. "I thought I could. I thought I could. I thought I could. I thought I could.

      I thought I could.

            I thought I could."